Buffalo Wings

by
Aaron Reynolds

illustrated by
Paulette Bogan

BLOOMSBURY
CHILDREN'S
BOOKS

Typeset in Kosmik Flipper and Big Limbo • Art created with watercolor • Book design by Alyssa Morris

Published by Bloomsbury U.S.A. Children's Books, 175 Fifth Avenue, New York, NY 10010
Distributed to the trade by Holtzbrinck Publishers

Library of Congress Cataloging-in-Publication Data
Reynolds, Aaron.
Buffalo wings / by Aaron Reynolds ; illustrated by Paulette Bogan. — 1st U.S. ed.
p.   cm.
Summary: While searching for the perfect Super Bowl snack, Rooster comes across a recipe for buffalo
wings and, before reading it completely, goes in search of what he believes is the missing ingredient.
ISBN-13: 978-1-59990-062-9 • ISBN-10: 1-59990-062-9 (hardcover)
ISBN-13: 978-1-59990-139-8 • ISBN-10: 1-59990-139-0 (reinforced)
[1. Roosters—Fiction. 2. Animals—Fiction. 3. Snack foods—Fiction.]
I. Bogan, Paulette, ill. II. Title.
PZ7.R33213Bu 2007   [E]—dc22   2006037024

First U.S. Edition 2007
Printed in China
2 4 6 8 10 9 7 5 3 1 (hardcover)
2 4 6 8 10 9 7 5 3 1 (reinforced)

All papers used by Bloomsbury U.S.A. are natural, recyclable products made from wood grown in well-managed
forests. The manufacturing processes conform to the environmental regulations of the country of origin.

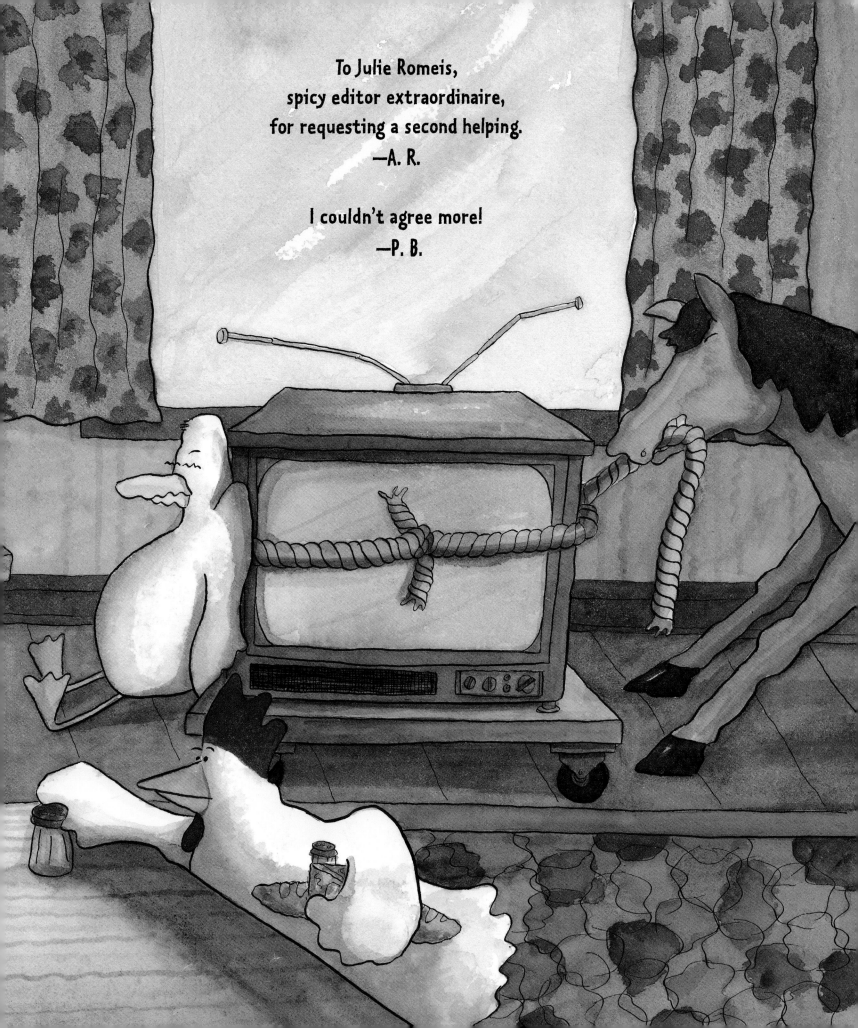

To Julie Romeis,
spicy editor extraordinaire,
for requesting a second helping.
—A. R.

I couldn't agree more!
—P. B.

It was the day of the big football game between the Mustangs and the Buffalos. The ducks dished up their famous quackamole. The pigs piled a platter knee-deep with nachos. And the horses heisted Farmer Nuthatcher's TV.

But in the henhouse of Nuthatcher Farm, something was missing.

The rooster had a hankering for a game-time snack with plenty of kick. Flipping through Mrs. Nuthatcher's cookbooks, he found the solution to his problem . . . **buffalo wings!**

Kickoff was close, so he skimmed the directions and mixed up a spicy, sassy sauce. But something was missing.

Of course! If the rooster wanted buffalo wings, he would have to find a buffalo.

Borrowing Farmer Nuthatcher's pickup truck, the rooster headed west—though nobody was quite certain where he learned to drive a stick shift.

WEST

Dreaming of wings, the rooster pulled the pickup into Buffalo Bob's Wild West Rodeo. He found bucking broncos and cowboy clowns.

But not a single buffalo.

Hot on the trail, the rooster steered toward Buffalo Smoke National Park.
He spied geysers and grizzly bears. But not a single buffalo.

Eager for the perfect football feast, the rooster cruised over to the Wild Buffalo Water Park. He spotted waterslides and wave pools. But not a single buffalo.

The gloomy rooster was heading for home when at last he spotted
a herd of buffalo in the fiery setting sun.
But something was missing.

Wings! The whole herd of buffalo was completely wing-free.
The rooster reread his recipe: garlic, vinegar, ketchup, hot
sauce, and . . .

... chicken wings!

The red-faced rooster closed the cookbook. His perfect feast was a flop.

But the herd invited the rooster to join their football festivities—though nobody was quite certain where they got the big-screen TV with surround sound.

The rooster chowed down on chuck-wagon chili.
He pigged out on Buffalo-style pizza with pineapple.
He inhaled outrageous onion rings.

But then the rooster discovered the jalapeño hush puppies.
Of course! The mouthwatering morsels were hot and spicy, with plenty of kick. The perfect game-time goodies!

The rooster was ready to head for home, hush puppies in hand.
But something was *still* missing.

His fiery football snack was no good without a game to go with it.
The rooster huddled his buffalo buddies and shared his plan.

Fired up, the rooster turned the truck toward Nuthatcher Farm.
They made a few stops along the way.

The next morning, the rooster organized the first-ever Nuthatcher
Farm football game. On the sidelines, there were mounds of munchies.
The ducks fixed quackamole. The pigs provided nachos.

The rooster whipped up jalapeño hush puppies, hot and spicy
with plenty of kick.
And nothing was missing.

But the rooster was too busy scoring a touchdown to notice.

Halftime Jalapeño Hush Puppies

2 jalapeño peppers

1¾ cups white cornmeal

1½ teaspoons salt

1 teaspoon baking powder

½ teaspoon baking soda

1 cup milk

1 egg, beaten

vegetable oil for frying

1. Cut jalapeño peppers in half. Remove and discard the seeds. Chop into very small pieces.

2. In a bowl, mix together cornmeal, salt, baking powder, and baking soda.

3. In another bowl, mix together milk and the egg. Mix together this wet stuff with the bowlful of dry stuff. Stir in the chopped jalapeños.

4. Pour 3 to 4 inches of oil into a saucepan. Heat the oil until it sizzles when you drop a small blob of batter into it.

5. Scoop the hush-puppy dough into the hot oil one spoonful at a time. Don't splash! Fry a few at a time, turning them once until golden brown, about 3 to 5 minutes. Remove them with a slotted spoon and put them on a paper towel to drain.

6. Dig in, but keep a glass of milk on the sidelines. These puppies pack a punch!